Dear Parents:

Congratulations! Your child is taking the first steps on an exciting journey. The destination? Independent reading!

STEP INTO READING® will help your child get there. The program offers five steps to reading success. Each step includes fun stories and colorful art or photographs. In addition to original fiction and books with favorite characters, there are Step into Reading Non-Fiction Readers, Phonics Readers and Boxed Sets, Sticker Readers, and Comic Readers—a complete literacy program with something to interest every child.

Learning to Read, Step by Step!

Ready to Read   Preschool–Kindergarten
• big type and easy words • rhyme and rhythm • picture clues
For children who know the alphabet and are eager to begin reading.

Reading with Help   Preschool–Grade 1
• basic vocabulary • short sentences • simple stories
For children who recognize familiar words and sound out new words with help.

Reading on Your Own   Grades 1–3
• engaging characters • easy-to-follow plots • popular topics
For children who are ready to read on their own.

Reading Paragraphs   Grades 2–3
• challenging vocabulary • short paragraphs • exciting stories
For newly independent readers who read simple sentences with confidence.

Ready for Chapters   Grades 2–4
• chapters • longer paragraphs • full-color art
For children who want to take the plunge into chapter books but still like colorful pictures.

STEP INTO READING® is designed to give every child a successful reading experience. The grade levels are only guides; children will progress through the steps at their own speed, developing confidence in their reading. The F&P Text Level on the back cover serves as another tool to help you choose the right book for your child.

Remember, a lifetime love of reading starts with a single step!

To my boys: thank you for one wild ride!
—D.D.

To teachers and librarians everywhere
—A.K.

Visit us on the Web!
StepIntoReading.com
rhcbooks.com

Educators and librarians, for a variety of teaching tools, visit us at RHTeachersLibrarians.com

Library of Congress Cataloging-in-Publication Data is available upon request.
ISBN 978-0-593-18046-4 (trade) — ISBN 978-0-593-18048-8 (lib. bdg.) —
ISBN 978-0-593-18047-1 (ebook)

Printed in the United States of America
10 9 8 7 6 5 4 3 2 1

This book has been officially leveled by using the F&P Text Level Gradient™ Leveling System.

Misty the Cloud
Fun Is in the Air

by Dylan Dreyer
with Alan Katz
illustrated by Rosie Butcher

Random House 🏠 New York

Clare and her mom
were having a picnic.
"It's so hot!" said Clare.

"I have an idea!"
said her mom.
"Let's go to
the beach!"

They packed up
the food and left.

They sat near the water.
Clare asked why
it was so much cooler
at the beach.

"The sun warms the sand and the air," said Clare's mom.

"Warm air rises. Then a cool breeze from the ocean replaces it.

"Warm air rising
is called an updraft.
It bounces
the air around
in the sky."

Big, puffy clouds
floated by.
"I'm sure
the clouds love
the updraft!" Clare said.

Clare was right!
Misty the Cloud
and her friends
were having
a great time
at the Sea Breeze
Carnival.

First, they all rode
the Updraft
Roller Coaster.

"Again!" said Nimby,
the littlest cloud.

They rode it again.

And again.

And again.

"Let's try the
bounce house!"
said Scud.

"House bounce!"
cheered Nimby.

Next, they went to
Mirror Land.

"Look, I'm a
mare's tail!"
said Wispy.

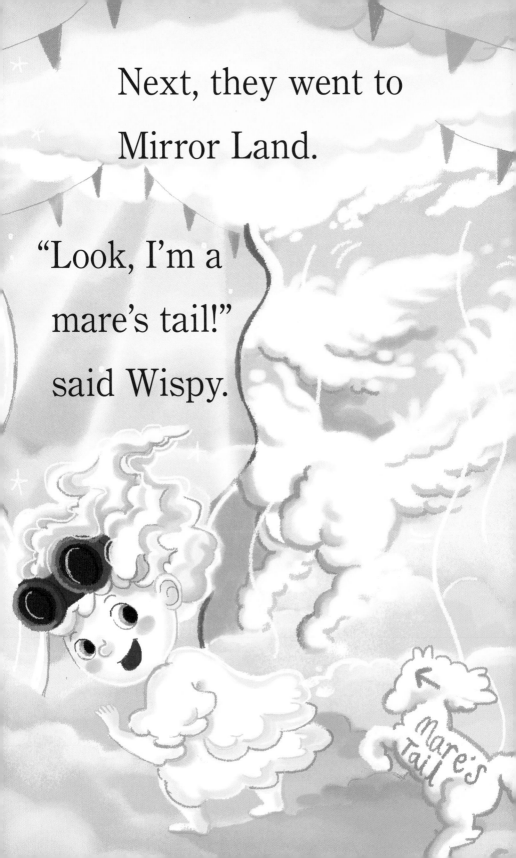

Mare's
Tail

"I'm an anvil!" said Kelvin.

"I'm Nimby!" said Nimby.

The clouds were having
so much fun.

They all lined up
for snacks.

"More, please!"
said Scud.

"More, please!"
said Wispy.

"More peas!"
said Nimby.

Next, the friends posed
behind funny cutouts.
"I'm a rock star,"
said Misty.
"I'm a clown,"
said Kelvin.

"I'm a football player,"
said Wispy.

"I'm a farmer,"
said Scud.

"Moo," said Nimby.

The sun was setting
at the beach.

The sea breeze
was almost gone.

At the carnival,
Misty and her friends
rode one final ride
as the sun set.

Clare thought
the beach was
the coolest place ever.
"Let's take a picture,"
said Clare.
"Say cheese!"

Misty thought
the carnival was
the coolest place ever.
"Let's take a picture,"
said Misty.
"Say cheese!"

"Peas!" Nimby said.